Magic Wagon

Content Consultant:
William Vicars, EdD, Director of Lifeprint Institute
and Associate Professor, ASL & Deaf Studies
California State University, Sacramento

by Dawn Babb Prochovnic
illustrated by Stephanie Bauer

The Best Day in Room A
Sign Language for School Activities

Story Time with Signs & Rhymes

visit us at www.abdopublishing.com

For Sara and Scott, honest critique partners, and for Stephanie, illustrator extraordinaire—DP
For two of the most wonderful kindergarten teachers on the planet, Theresa Cumpston and Ann Fordney—SB

Published by Magic Wagon, a division of the ABDO Group, 8000 West 78th Street, Edina, Minnesota 55439.
Copyright © 2010 by Abdo Consulting Group, Inc. International copyrights reserved in all countries. All rights reserved. No part of this book may be reproduced in any form without written permission from the publisher.

Looking Glass Library™ is a trademark and logo of Magic Wagon.

Printed in the United States.

♻ PRINTED ON RECYCLED PAPER

Written by Dawn Babb Prochovnic
Illustrations by Stephanie Bauer
Edited by Stephanie Hedlund and Rochelle Baltzer
Cover and Interior layout and design by Neil Klinepier

Story Time with Signs & Rhymes provides an introduction to ASL vocabulary through stories that are written and structured in English. ASL is a separate language with its own structure. Just as there are personal and regional variations in spoken and written languages, there are similar variations in sign language.

Library of Congress Cataloging-in-Publication Data
Prochovnic, Dawn Babb.
  The best day in room A : sign language for school activities / by Dawn Babb Prochovnic ; illustrated by Stephanie Bauer ; content consultant, William Vicars.
      p. cm. -- (Story time with signs & rhymes)
  Includes "alphabet handshapes;" American Sign Language glossary, fun facts, and activities; further reading and web sites.
  ISBN 978-1-60270-667-5
 [1. Stories in rhyme. 2. Schools--Fiction. 3. Counting. 4. American Sign Language. 5. Vocabulary.] I. Bauer, Stephanie, ill. II. Title.
  PZ8.3.P93654Bes 2009
  [E]--dc22
                                                            2009002380

Alphabet Handshapes

American Sign Language (ASL) is a visual language that uses handshapes, movements, and facial expressions. Sometimes people spell English words by making the handshape for each letter in the word they want to sign. This is called fingerspelling. The pictures below show the handshapes for each letter in the manual alphabet.

Room A

On the first day in Room A,
we learned to count to one
with one treasure box.
And our class chanted, "**Learning** is fun!"

learn

On the second day in Room A,
we learned to count to two
with two noisy drums and one treasure box.
And our class chanted, "**Drumming** is fun!"

drum

On the third day in Room A,
we learned to count to three
with three picture books, two noisy drums,
and one treasure box.
And our class chanted, "**Reading** is fun!"

read

9

On the fourth day in Room A,
we learned to count to four
with four yellow smocks, three picture books,
two noisy drums, and one treasure box.
And our class chanted, "**Painting** is fun!"

paint

On the fifth day in Room A,
we learned to count to five
with five shiny pots, four yellow smocks,
three picture books, two noisy drums,
and one treasure box.
And our class chanted, "**Cooking** is fun!"

cook

On the sixth day in Room A,
we learned to count to six
with six colored pens, five shiny pots,
four yellow smocks, three picture books,
two noisy drums, and one treasure box.
And our class chanted, "**Writing** is fun!"

14

write

On the seventh day in Room A,
we learned to count to seven
with seven rubber balls, six colored pens,
five shiny pots, four yellow smocks,
three picture books, two noisy drums, and one treasure box.
And our class chanted, "**Bouncing** is fun!"

bounce

On the eighth day in Room A,
we learned to count to eight
with eight wooden blocks, seven rubber balls,
six colored pens, five shiny pots, four yellow smocks,
three picture books, two noisy drums, and one treasure box.
And our class chanted, "**Building is fun!**"

19

On the ninth day in Room A,
we learned to count to nine
with nine tiny seeds, eight wooden blocks,
seven rubber balls, six colored pens, five shiny pots,
four yellow smocks, three picture books, two noisy drums,
and one treasure box. And our class chanted, **"Planting is fun!"**

Plant

21

On the best day in Room A,
we learned to **count** to ten
with ten silver dimes,
nine tiny seeds,
eight wooden blocks,
seven rubber balls,

10

9

8

7

count

six colored pens, five shiny pots, four yellow smocks, three picture books, two noisy drums, and one treasure box.

21

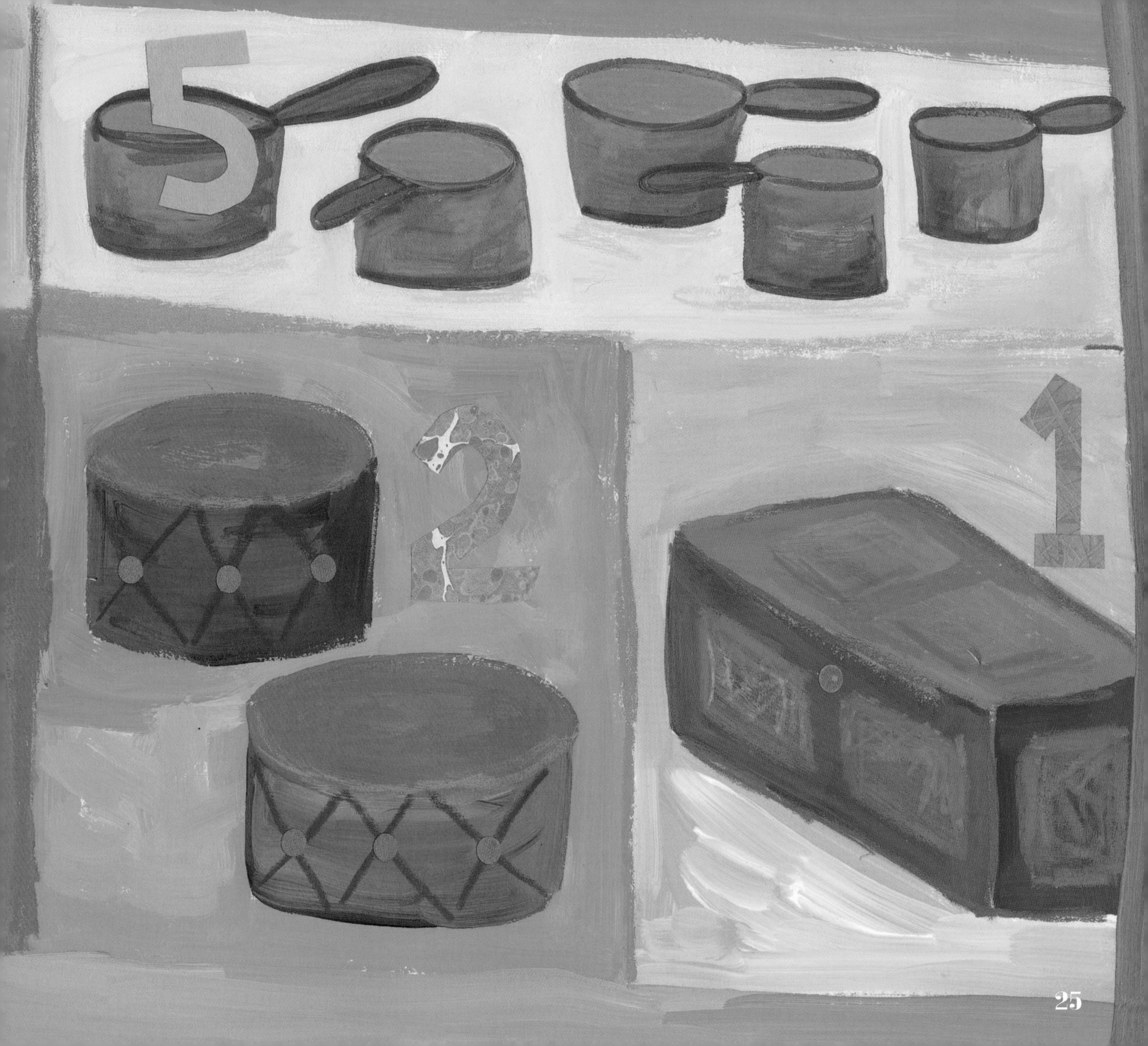
5
2
1

And our class shouted, "**Counting** is fun!"

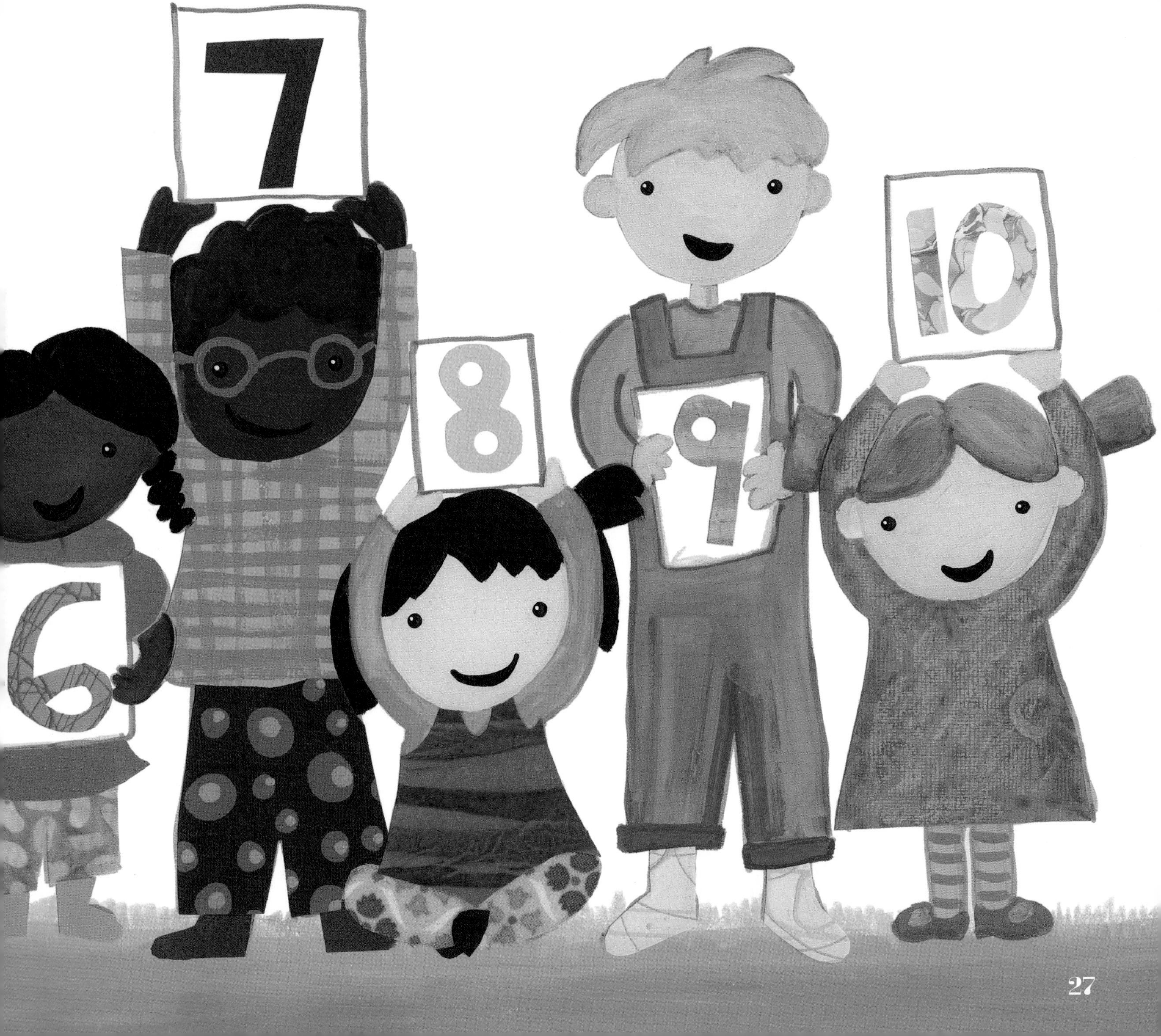
6
7
8
9
10

American Sign Language Glossary

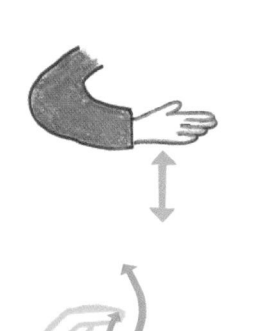

bounce: Hold one hand in front of you with your palm facing down and your elbow bent. Now move your hand up and down several times. It should look like you are bouncing a ball in front of you.

build: Hold your hands in front of your chest with your palms facing down and your fingers bent at the knuckle. Begin with the tips of your right fingers gently resting on the tips of your left fingers then put your left fingers on top of your right. Continue in an alternating motion, gradually moving your hands up toward your head. It should look like you are layering blocks on top of each other.

cook: Hold your hands in front of you with the fingers of your right hand resting on the palm of your left hand and your palms facing each other. Now quickly flip your right hand over so your right palm is facing up. It should look like you are flipping a pancake in a frying pan.

count: Touch the pointer finger and thumb of your right "F Hand" to the palm of your left hand near your wrist. Now slide your pointer finger and thumb across the palm of your left hand until you reach your fingertips. It should look like you are counting small objects that are lined up on the palm of your hand.

drum: Hold your fists in front of you with your palms facing in and your pointer fingers slightly extended at the knuckle. Now move your hands up and down in front of your chest by bending at the wrist in an alternating motion. It should look like you are using drumsticks to beat a drum.

learn: Touch the fingers and thumb of your right hand to the palm of your left hand. Now press the fingers of your right hand to your thumb as you move your hand up and touch your forehead. It should look like you are taking information from a book and moving it into your brain.

paint: Hold your hands in front of you with your palms facing each other and your fingertips touching. Drag the fingers of your right hand down the palm of your left hand to your wrist. Now bend the fingers of your right hand at the knuckle and drag the backs of your fingertips up the palm of your left hand, then repeat. It should look like you are making brushstrokes with a paintbrush.

plant: Hold your flattened "O Hand" near your shoulder with your palm facing down then rub your thumb across your fingers and move into an "A Hand." Now repeat this movement with a slightly forward motion. It should look like you are holding little seeds and dropping them into the ground.

read: Hold your hands to the side of your body with your palms facing each other and your right "V Hand" pointing at the top of your left palm. Now slide the fingertips of your right "V Hand" to the bottom of your left palm. It should look like your eyes are moving down the page as you read a book.

write: Hold your left hand in front of you with your palm facing up. Now press your pointer finger and thumb of your right hand together and touch them to the palm of your left hand near your wrist. Then move your right hand across the palm of your left hand toward your fingertips in a wiggly motion. It should look like you are holding a pen and writing with it.

Fun Facts about ASL

A *writer* is a person who writes, and a *painter* is a person who paints. In ASL, you can add a special sign called an "agent affix" or a "person affix" to some verbs to show that you are talking about a person who does a particular action. To do this, hold both hands in front of the shoulders with palms facing each other and fingers pointing out. Then move your hands down toward your waist. It should look like you are making a straight outline of a person standing in front of you. To sign "painter," make the sign for "paint" then make the special "person affix" sign.

Most sign language dictionaries describe how a sign looks for a right-handed signer. If you are left-handed, you would modify the instructions so the signs feel more comfortable to you. For example, to sign "write," a left-handed signer would hold the right hand in front of the body and make the writing motion with the left hand.

Signing is fun to learn and can be helpful in many ways. Kids who sign often become better readers and stronger spellers than kids who don't sign. Even babies can learn to use sign language to communicate before they can talk. And when you learn to sign, you can communicate with many people who are deaf.

Signing Activities

Count to Ten Circle Game: Stand in a circle and choose someone to go first. The first player makes the sign for the number "one." The second player makes the sign for the number "two." Play continues with each player making the sign for the next number in sequence all the way up to ten. The player that signs "ten" must jump in place anywhere between one and five times then sit down. The player that goes next must start counting with the next number. So, if the player before them jumped five times, they would make the sign for "six." Play continues until everyone is sitting down.

Spell and Sign Circle Game: List the glossary words on the board, then sit in a circle. Choose someone to go first. The first player selects a word from the glossary then makes the handshape for the first letter in that word. The second player makes the handshape for the next letter in the word. When the word has been completely spelled, the last player must make the sign for the word. Any player who cannot sign the correct word on their turn is out and must move away from the circle. Play continues with a new word from the glossary until all words have been spelled and signed, or until there is only one player left.

Write Your Own Story: Select five words from the glossary that you want to practice. Write a creative story using those five words. Now read your story to a partner. When you come to one of the words from the glossary, make the sign for that word!

Additional Resources

Further Reading

Costello, Elaine, PhD. *Random House Webster's Concise American Sign Language Dictionary*. Bantam, 2002.

Heller, Lora. *Sign Language for Kids*. Sterling, 2004.

Sign2Me. *Pick Me Up! Fun Songs for Learning Signs (A CD and Activity Guide)*. Northlight Communications, 2003.

Warner, Penny. *Signing Fun*. Gallaudet University Press, 2006.

Web Sites

To learn more about ASL, visit ABDO Group online at **www.abdopublishing.com**. Web sites about ASL are featured on our Book Links page. These links are routinely monitored and updated to provide the most current information available.